I0646935

umSinsi Press
PO Box 28129
Malvern
4055
Kwa-Zulu Natal
South Africa

web: http://www.umsinsi.com

ISBN 1-86900-674-7

FACES

**Free Spirit Dancing Pencils
Writing Club**

About the Authors

Valarie Chetty

Valarie Chetty is a dynamic young writer who loves all things creative. She is also a fashion designer and an educator. She sees herself as an eternal student and has a variety of interests, from Anthropology, which allows her to travel and immerse herself in different cultures, to Faerie Lore. She believes that you're never too old – or too young – to learn something new.

Her first book, *A Magical Mission*, was an adventure in fantasy, which explored the realms of magic and mystery. In this book she explores the depths of the human condition.

Shenaaz Khan

Shenaaz Khan is fascinated by the mysteries of life. Her interests include delving into astrology and immersing herself in the beauty of nature. Her writing comes straight from the heart and is inspired by her own life experiences, which have shaped her into the wonderful person she has become.

"I still consider Love to be the greatest mystery of all. I will spend the rest of my life trying to solve its puzzles."

Indira Gilbert

Indira Gilbert is married and has four children. She has travelled extensively and worked with people from different cultures. Her experience as a Social Worker has a bearing on her writing: through her writing she hopes to lead people to understanding the human nature.

Indira has written two non-fiction books: *Handbook for Parents, & Handbook for Teens*.

Veena Narainen

Veena Narainen is an inspirational Human and Social Sciences educator at Queensburgh Girls High. Her desire for writing poetry and short stories are fuelled by a passion for sharing her extensive knowledge about our heritage and the rich and diverse cultures in our country.

She lives in Queensburgh, Durban with her husband and two children.

Contents

The
Beauty
of
Creation,

Our inspiration...

NATURE
By Indira Gilbert

Patter of tiny feet
Innocently running around
On the freshly mowed, green lawn.
Jumping on the heaps of raked grass.
Fun to play with
Fun to jump on
Fun to roll on
And throw oneself on.

Nature can be fun
As is created.
Parks with trees, flowers, grass
Provide fun for all,
A home for Creation.
The birds and the bees.

Home for some
Fun for some
Leisure for some
Jobs for some.
Creation is provided.
The rest is up to man's imagination.

A NEEDLE IN A HAYSTACK
By Indira Gilbert

It is a strange feeling to consider oneself insignificant in life. In this somewhat overpopulated world, one can easily feel like a 'needle in a haystack' where nobody is concerned about, or even considers one's existence – one's experiences, pain, joy, needs, or wants.

When one passes on from this life, life continues without a dent as though the individual who passed on never existed. The individual is soon forgotten. A good, meaningful, valuable contribution then seems no different from a life lived selfishly.

On the other side of this coin are the beauty, uniqueness and importance of an individual to those in his 'world': neighbours, family, friends and colleagues. The lives of those in contact with the individual *can* be imprinted. A simple, unique, other-centred life determines and shapes the lives of those around him/her, especially the dependents that live and experience life by what is taught through word and deed.

Yes, one's influence does live on …. through the lives of one's children, and is carried over from one generation to another. What an impact!

Small things in life are important: they are very important. Although the effects may not be seen in great works, discoveries, or inventions, it is felt in the heart; in the place that matters most. And it does leave its mark for generations to come.

So the needle in the haystack does have a purpose and is 'felt': the thinness and smallness of the needle and the sharpness of the point does leave its mark.

Yes, we can make a difference in life - in the life of at least one individual, and in this way, impact on many more. We may not be acknowledged while we are alive, or even when we are dead; we may not even be remembered by the next generation, but the mark will remain and be carried on from one generation to another.

It is an exciting thought that we can actually affect generations to come without even being involved in any great invention or discovery. What an opportunity! What a life! What an impact!

And yet, amidst all Creation, how extremely tiny is one life!

THE SEA
by Indira Gilbert

The sea
So calming, so relaxing,
A means of escape.
While watching the mighty roaring waves,
All else is forgotten
In its presence.
It's becomes overwhelming,
Overbearing,
It overtakes everything that comes its way.

Yet,
What a source of inspiration it is,
Of joy,
Of fun,
And excitement,
To all,
Everywhere!

Life is begat by it,
Life is taken by it.
Fun is provided by it,
Fun is abruptly ended by it.

It is there for man's pleasure
But must be submitted to.

What a Creation!

Memories made
Of good and bad,
Of bringing loved ones together,
And of ripping loved ones apart.
Of generating romance,
And ending it.

What a Creation!

PUPPIES
By Indira Gilbert

What sources of inspiration puppies are!

While engrossed in each other's company, nothing else seems to matter to them. There is no need for life to be structured. They sleep when they need to, are ready to respond to their owner at any time, and completely give themselves to one another.

Anything can become a source of fun and entertainment to them – a leaf, or a plastic packet blowing in the wind, a mat that provides a bed, or a bird that has come to eat off the ground.

No mountain seems *insurmountable to them*: a huge barking dog, the highest wall are a couple of their challenges. A puppy seems to consider in his mind, that it can overcome. Or is it their way of saying to its owner 'I am here for you. No one can attack you.'

The freedom enjoyed by puppies is *balanced* by submission to their owner. All commands and demands are adhered to. Yet out of sight of the owner, the excitement of breaking some of the very commands like 'digging up in the garden' forms the basis of their enjoyment.

Puppies provide a lesson for us on how to live our lives: caring for those who love us while not allowing this to determine or destroy our lifestyle.

Puppies do surely know how to have fun!
Do we know how to have fun while keeping ourselves needed, wanted, and loved?

***

Perseverance
By Valarie Chetty

Each day starts with its arms stretching
outward,
Aching to touch the sky,
Wondrous beauty,
Immeasurable anticipation.
It reaches the summit,
And realises it can go no further.
All hope, all faith,
All dissipates
Into blackened melancholy.
But all is not lost,
For she rises again
And starts over with a hope renewed.

Inside me
By Valarie Chetty

Look inside
These windows of my soul.
Fly over the dusty boards
And cobwebbed floors.
Come past this lonely, dreary, dark place.

And deep inside,
Past the muddy pools
Of murky waters,
And tainted mirrors
Of my mind.
Past all the devious facades,
And distant memories.

You will find,
A little flicker of light.
Trapped inside,
Trying to break free,
And fly straight out of me,
Wanting to come home to Thee.

Imagination
By Valarie Chetty

I'm floating,
On a sea of clouds,
But no substance to catch me if I fall.
A sea of marshmallows,
Soft comforting and surreal.
I'm going somewhere,
But nowhere?
Where is this somewhere?
Where am I going?

I don't know how long I've been floating,
dreaming, flying.
There is no concept of time.
There is no time,
But it feels like forever.
Just fluffy, sugar spun clouds of soft
nothing....forever.

Pink, lavender, lilac, blue, yellow, silvery hues.
All blending into each other like a pastel lake,
Drowning into itself.
Dashes and swirls,
Like a Van Gogh dream.

My imagination takes me to the highest clouds
That float above the oceans and the
mountains,
Places that resonate with marvellous sounds.

I've been to places you can only see
With your eyes shut,
A Wiccan circle,
And a Zulu hut.

I see only things I want to see,
Because this is the only place,
That I can be free.

***

The Rising Sun
By Shenaaz Khan

Darkness gives way to light
A soft orange glow
Emerges, slowly, out of the night
Close by, water gently flows

Beauty and peace surround me
As I gaze in awe
At a sunrise, so free
Of any flaw
Hope arrives with the dawn
A chance for a new day
My sadness, despair, all gone
I bow my head and pray .

Lights,
By Shenaaz Khan

Lights, multi – hued, shimmer and dance
In a haze of Ethereal beauty

The silken strands of the web
Each delicate strand attaches
To itself a beauty that's
Not breathtaking, not harsh
But something that's pure and spiritual

The complexities of the Maker
And the complete web
Completely rainbow coloured
When dancing in the light breeze
And catching the rays of the sun

The different shades of happiness
A quiet, subtle kind of joy
Bursting at the seams
But not loud, not very visible
Not the kind to shout about
But certainly something to smile about

The radiance that is incandescent

A feeling of lightness airiness
Floating, but yet never not solid
The nature of joy almost fey
Like something from another world

The land of fairies, gnomes

Where all things are magic
Where the mirror reflects light
And you wonder where the darkness
Ever came from
It seems so far away

Like heaven, yet the joy
Does not bubble forth
It stays contained and just keeps on floating
Moving, peacefully
Bringing content, bringing a sense of safety

Is this it then ?
Is this the right thing
Does stability fade off
After a time
Do we look for
Excitement .

***

What is life,
If not for a
Meaningful
Existence?

A Journey through my mind
By Valarie Chetty

Milky way…
Swirling galaxies…
Stephen hawking…
All boggling my mind.
The where of origin?
Nowhere inside,
Somewhere outside.
Swirling, swirling,
Getting dizzy.
Flurry, flurry, flying free.
It's something inside of me!
Tomorrow is a new day,
A new problem.
Only solutions to find,
For everyone else.
So much to do,
So little time.
Everything's moving so fast,
So near, so long,
So dizzy…
It makes no sense.
I'm running out of ink,
But nothing to write.
The mission of a genius,
To find something surreal,

Something wildly fundamental,
Functional, beautiful.
Useful beauty,
What is that?
A hundred red roses,
Cut from growing plants,
Bleeding, thorny,
Hating scissors.
Crying and dying,
Representing love.
Whose love?
Who's to say,
What
Where
How
Why
The world is so???
Tell me what you know.
The earth is round,
A spherical ball.
Swirling somewhere deep
In a mystical hall,
Of black nothingness
All around.
A lonely, desolate ball,
Spinning, flying, circling the sun,
Round and round and
round and round.

I'm still dizzy.
STOP!

I can't take it anymore!
Give me a purpose.
Something easy,
Not to save the world,
Not to change a nation,
Not to change myself,
Something easy,
Mowing the lawn – maybe?
Only time can tell,
What the hell
I'm doing here.
My heart is full of nonsense,
My head is full of blood.
Thinking of all the wars on earth,
The stars in the sky,
The water on Mars,
Why do so many people have to die?
Why fight for peace,
Kill for freedom
And long for doom?
My lens sees only inverted pictures
Of what should be,
Not what really is.
Only illusion, delusion and grandeur.
Psycho-para-neuroticism,

What does that mean?
Sounds interesting
And genius-like,
But really nothing
But juxtaposed half-meanings,
Incomplete babblings of an untrained mind.
Unbridled, unrestrained,
Completely passionate and wild.
A wild horse galloping through the desert,
Like a nightmare through the sky,
Terribly blinding and fiercely frightening.
It's only my mind,

It's only me.

I'm just terrified of how much I can be.

Lessons I have learned over the years...
By Valarie Chetty

About myself:

1. There's no such thing as *normal,* only other people's perceptions of what normal is, so never try to fit in by changing the person you are inside.
2. Accept yourself completely. You don't need to apologise for who you are, only the wrongs you have done.
3. Intelligence is not a precursor for success.
4. Always choosing the path of least resistance means giving up the opportunity to learn and grow.
5. Every moment, whether good or bad, is just temporary.
6. Always reminiscing about the past or planning for the future robs you of the precious present.
7. Being number one often means being on your own.
8. If you can't say anything good, keep your mouth shut. Don't stick your foot in it!
9. Don't try to change the world, inspire the world with the way you live your life.
10. Learn to take it easy. Life is not heart surgery!

11. Let the Universe deals with life's inequalities. You don't need to exact revenge on another being.

12. Apologise when you do something wrong, it cleanses the soul and relieves it.

13. Your perception of the world is just that, a single view of absolute reality. Sometimes you need to step back and take a look at the bigger picture.

14. Don't force your will upon the Universe. Let your future unfold like the petals of a flower in accordance with the laws of nature.

15. Wait. Patience has to be learnt.

16. Thoughts have energy. The beginning of a thought is the building of a pathway for the map of your future.

17. Sometimes what you want from God is not what God wants for you. Learn to accept it.

18. Pass your time doing something useful. Don't waste time waiting for the right time.

19. Take time out each day to do something wonderful, like plucking a flower or singing in the shower.

20. We all bugger up now and again, but the world goes on turning without batting an eyelid, so don't be too hard on yourself.

About other people:

1. People only disappoint you when you have too high expectations of them. Expect nothing and you will be pleasantly surprised by them.
2. One person really can make a difference to the world, even if nobody else knows about it.
3. It is always better to give than to horde.
4. Common sense is hard to come by.
5. Friends are good therapists.
6. Never call or email someone when you're really angry – especially not your boss!
7. You may pride yourself on being brutally honest, but not everyone can always handle your version of the truth. Sometimes, you need to water it down and add lots of sugar to it.
8. Love grows exponentially.
9. Try to stop insulting people. It just shows how flawed you really are when you try to make yourself look good by insulting others.

10. If you really want to be admired, lift others to greater heights. Give people room to be themselves and make their own mistakes.
11. When people steal something from you, forgive them. When you die, you're not going to be taking it with you anyway.
12. If someone really wants your advice, they will ask for it.
13. Try hard to listen to others. They might have something useful to say that could change your life, even if it is only one word.
14. A little compliment goes a long way.
15. Every time you say something that hurts another person, you start a spark of hatred in yourself and in them.
16. Life is too short to harbour a grudge – especially against a stupid person.
17. Life would be too boring if we were all the same. Celebrate people's differences.
18. You don't have to understand other people's cultures, just respect them.
19. Preaching your beliefs and practising them are two completely different things. People want to see you do good not hear you say how good you are.
20. We are all fragments of an infinite soul.

About being a teacher:

1. Life is the best teacher so empower your
    students to be able to live their own lives.
2. Knowledge without purpose is just useless
    information.
3. Life is not all about punctuation and
    spelling. Not every child will grow up to
    be a copywriter or an editor. Try to focus
    on what is truly important in life.
4. Give your children room to grow and
    explore their interests in the classroom.
5. A quiet classroom is not an indication that
    learning is taking place. You may need to
    check if some pupils are still awake!
6. Be like a soft cushion instead of an
    abrasive steel brush. Give children the
    opportunity to bounce back instead of
    scraping away their layers of self-worth.
7. It is difficult to teach when nobody wants
    to learn, but even if there is just one child
    that wants to learn, know that you efforts
    are not in vain. Focus on the one budding
    flower than the hundreds of thorns that
    surround it.
8. There will be days when you question the
    value of your work and there will be days

when you need to question the work of your values.

9. The moments I remember most vividly from my own school days were definitely not about taking down notes from the board or a textbook!

10. Love is free from religion, class, caste and creed, especially in the classroom.

11. Teaching is a learning process. It is also a process of nurturing – the best in others and in yourself.

12. See your classroom as a garden. Each child is like a little seed. You can treat them all the same but at the end of the day they will each grow up to be different. Some may be flowers and some may bear fruit. Others may provide shade and shelter while some may even grow to become weeds. You will never know what each will turn out to be until long after they've left your hands so treat all the same while you have them. Don't kill a rose before it blooms.

13. Problems and obstacles are blessings. Getting through it opens up a road for others. That is true guidance.

14. Dexterity and ability are not for praise. They are for purpose.

15. Knowing more than others is not a sign of superiority. No knowledge is new knowledge. You can't own it - it belongs to the Universe. We can all tap into it. It's how you use it that counts.
16. Don't focus on awards, focus on how your work has helped others or made a difference in the world.
17. True achievement is when something you do makes a difference, for the better and however small, in someone else's life.
18. A feeling of accomplishment is a feeling of usefulness.
19. Don't overwhelm yourself. Take baby steps, or crawl if you have to!
20. Believe that magical things can happen.

Soul-Searching
By Valarie Chetty

I cannot live with the loneliness of the stars,
Only faded light,
Far from home and no life.
They don't even exist,
Yet we see them.
They guide us and give us hope,
But even they,
Are dead.
It is only an illusion,
Just like life is only an illusion,
That we create for ourselves.
We aren't really living,
Merely existing.
Empty shells dying with every moment,
And every moment brings the nothingness
closer.

There is always something,
Something outside ourselves,
That we clutch and grab at,
To give us peace,
To give us hope,
But the effort is futile,
For nothing outside us can fill us up
On the inside.

Find what's somewhere deep inside,
Beyond the dark crevices of your mind,
Beyond the sea of your soul,
And there you will truly find,
Something to fill the deep hole
And free you from your earthly confine.

Woman's Lament
By Valarie Chetty

I wake up and creep slowly out of my tent. I stand and take a deep breath in. The air is cold and piercing, yet refreshing. I can hear the crispy, curled brown leaves nestling on the dew-wet grass as they crackle under my leather boots. The old women of the village have begun their morning chores. Collecting and boiling water, making breakfast and tidying up the yards while the little children and their fathers sleep inside the warm woven tents.

It was hard work and the strain could be seen on every one of their leathery faces but they never complained. They always did their duty, they always did what they were expected to do, with complete submission and not an ounce of revolt.

I look at them and think to myself, "Is this all there is?"

I can't stand it anymore! How can I grow up and become this? I want to find out what's beyond the hills and valleys. Is there life after buffalo hunting? There must be so much more, I feel it in my bones!

It feels like everything inside me wants to burst out of me and roam free. There's such a rush, such excitement and such a hurry – but to go where?

This place is blinding, binding, suffocating and choking.

The smoke from the fires outside each little tent wafts through the air and reminds me that I have chores to do, mouths to feed and clothes to mend before I go out and conquer the world.

*****

Power Of Dreams
By Shenaaz Khan

Do you know the strength of water ?
Yet you cannot grasp it in your hands.
Of course, you can contain it
In a container of any shape
Or size.
Water is so easily adaptable
To its holder.
Without water one cannot live.
It could also very easily kill you.
Its flow is fluid and it has
A strength that is not solid.
It can be heated, it can
Be frozen
Even if thrown away,
It goes on flowing
Sometimes it is dirty
We recycle it for use
Yet water is a cleanser
We cannot kill water
It forms into vapour
Comes down as rain
Flows in rivers, stagnates
In ponds

And moves back and forth
In mighty waves on the sea
Such is the spirit of dreams
That cannot be destroyed.

Pizza Fizzah
By Shenaaz Khan

The little dark haired girl had a doll in her arms, she suddenly abandoned the doll and started dancing. She really loved to dance. Anyone could tell by the expression on her face and the lightness of her feet. She twirled around, smiling happily, in her own private world, where she and the music were the only things that mattered.

Suddenly, the moment of ecstasy was shattered, when her brother, launched himself at her, punching her in the head, in the face, anywhere he could land his blows, unthinking, uncaring.

He was pulled away by their mother, who was very angry with him. In those few brief moments, the little girl's mood had changed. Now she was crying loudly, running toward her brother, attacking him, trying to kick him and bite him at the same time. Once more, a tired and angry mom had to play referee.

"You are not my friend ", the little girl told her brother. When I am a big girl, I won't buy a house and car for you." Her brother let out a roar, but was restrained by Mom again.

Soon, the little girl picked up her doll again. The contrast was quite striking between the fair-haired doll and the dark-haired girl.

The child was as lovely as any doll. She held her doll tightly to her, and comforted it saying, "Don't cry baby, Mommy's here. Now go to sleep, please dodo, baby, dodo."

She forgave her brother later when he said he was sorry, and with a sweet smile, she cuddled up to him and kissed him on the cheek. "I love my brother," she said.

My name is Fizzah, call me Pizza Fizzah.

Old – Time
By Shenaaz Khan

Our lives are
Dominated by time
We can't escape
The restrictions
Every waking moment
Is spent in a rush
There's no time
For relaxation
And fun
Always at the back
Of our minds.
What's the time ?

***

My Mother's Hands
By Veena Narainen

My mother's hands were special. They were small but strong. Her beautifully tapered fingers were always neatly manicured that one would have thought that she was a lady of leisure rather than a busy mother of six growing children.

I never failed to marvel at the variety of tasks her hands accomplished , especially when we were young. She would rise early every morning to make fresh rotis (Indian hand made bread) and delicious fillings because my dad would not have his lunch any other way. When we awoke , we would immediately be lifted up by floury hands and kissed excitedly on the cheeks. It was as if she'd seen us after a very long time and had been pining for us. This happened every morning for a long time.

The evenings were equally enjoyable , if not better. My sister Saras and I, being the youngest, would languish in her warm lap, while she would tell us intriguing stories of the past. Dad would sip his coffee while relaxing on his favourite green couch and the glimmer in his eyes would tell me that he had joined in the fantasy. When mother dragged her fingers across my face , I would giggle and squeeze my eyes shut when they passed down my nose and cross over my gaping mouth. Soon I would be asleep after her fingers made furrows through my hair.

'You have healing hands', Mrs Naidoo , the old lady next door used to tell mother. 'Even I don't have that magic touch when it comes to healing children's wounds.' Mother would laugh modestly and say that as far as she knew all the women in her family, as far down to her great , great grandmother, had special hands. As a pampered six year old, I strongly believed this to be true. I have often witnessed how mother would have to play doctor to the children of the neighbourhood. One incident stands firm in my memory.

My sisters Rekha and Priya were playing in the playground next to our home with their friends. My mother was convinced that Rekha should have been a boy since she was very rough in her demeanour and was aptly called 'the Rek', but on this occasion having spotted a group of well-known boys on the playground, she conjured up her all feminine wiles, hoping to impress the disinterested group who seemed to be more engrossed in the earthy composition under their shoes rather than the bunch of giggling girls.

To draw their attention which seemed more of an irritating task rather than an exciting opportunity, she challenged the girls to a race down a slightly steep slope nearby , but the urgency to impress was too overwhelming for Rekha who tore off to an early start just before the other girls reached the top. What followed were screams of excruciating pain as she tumbled rather unceremoniously to the bottom. She had cut her leg on a broken piece of bottle.

We could not decide whether it was the huge cut on her leg or the embarrassment of revealing her bright red panties that tore when she fell, that caused her to howl uncontrollably. Eventually it was only mother's reassuring voice and comforting hands that eased her pain and stifled her sobs of humiliation.

Rekha had grown in into a beautiful young lady since that incident and not only did she change but dad also changed. He had been in and out of jobs , taken to drinking uncontrollably and there were whispers of another woman. We would no longer cling merrily to mother or languish on her warm lap. Instead we would spend our time sitting in silence or pretending to fiddle around with some important activity in our rooms. Mother would spend much of her time grumbling and brooding like a restless hen and would often fling the kitchen utensils when she was beset by some enraging thoughts. I guessed it was the unknown woman or the drinking or both.

However I longed to see her smile at me or just smile but it was a rare sight if it would ever happen. With every passing day the brightness of her complexion was replaced by lines of stress and misery. It was a scary thing to approach her when she was in this temperament for she never hesitated to swing her hands across your face with a hard slap if your request seemed ridiculous or impertinent.

And so we remained , sheltered like refugees in our rooms because of dad. I hated him. It was because of him that she had become like this.

He would often stay away from work for long periods of time and spend much of his time in the pubs. Mother would froth and fume like a brewing storm as she paced around meaninglessly around the house. I hated to see her this way. She often looked hagged, her long hair falling in an unkempt fashion around her puffy face. The sight of her clothes that hung loosely on her tired body saddened me. I suggested once that she wear her favourite pink silk dress, but she waved me off impatiently and refused to have her hair plaited neatly by Saras. My misery , like hers continued to grow and the absence of my brothers and older sisters , who went off to stay with distant relatives, made it even harder to get through each day.

I had grown accustomed to hearing quiet sobs coming from her room but I could only peep in because I feared her temper and melancholic moods. What had gone wrong? As if reading my thoughts , the answer to this question would barge into the house like an ogre an its captives. Often he would fall supine on the lounge floor in a drunken stupor and Saras would rush to him in a frightened hysteria , tug at his jacket to see if he were still breathing. Mother would pull her away in a fit of rage while I would hide behind the sofa fearing what would come next.

"You wretched woman!" he would yell with wide-eyed anger and spit flying out of his mouth like venom from a snake. "You miserable woman!"... That was enough for mother, but before she could get away he would rise up with renewed strength and grasp her by the hair, swing her around and bang her head against the wall. She would scream but it was often our yells and pleading watery eyes that saved her from becoming a fleshy pulp.

I missed school often in the days that followed since there was no one to take care of mother. When morning came she wanted to lie in her bed as if she were dead and I often wished that she were because she was in a pallid state already. I would go quietly to the room and draw the curtains but she would turn her face away from the light and cover the purplish – blue bruises under the duvet in her dark world. I had grown accustomed to that and her rejection of tea and other comfort that was offered to her , but deep within I hoped that it would be different.

Accomplishing the household tasks was a feat due to my clumsiness and inexperience , for I had just turned eleven. But I did not fail to notice the neglected conditions in which we lived. The haphazard arrangements of the rooms , the smell of misery and melancholy manifested through the dusty furniture and dirty walls seemed to enhance our suffering.

Even the once bright yellow kitchen walls, like our faces, faded into a dull jaundiced hue. Nevertheless, Saras and I tried our best to nurse mother back to health , hoping to see perhaps just a glimmer of hope on her face. But it was not to be. The beatings and abuse continued.

Mother remained frail, her hands remained frail. She had lost any desire to do the things she once enjoyed. When I held them, they seemed weightless and dead already so that I often wished I could infuse fresh blood into the veins that stuck out like tiny rivulets.

Many seasons had passed and one Christmas my brothers and sisters came home to visit. Saras and I were ecstatic. Rekha had grown taller and more beautiful , Priya boasted of a possible love interest and my brothers looking handsome and lithe with closely cropped hair, jeans and t-shirt, certainly lifted most of the gloom. They had just started to work now and had huge dreams for all of us.

Saras and I listened with rapt interest and it seemed fantastical like the stories mother used to tell us. We were nevertheless transported into a different world far away from our misery. What swept us away was also the food. My sisters slaved over the stove for hours laughing, giggling and concocting the most delicious and colourful dishes I have ever seen.

We helped as well, tasting, messing but having ever so much of fun. I wished that everyday would be like that. When they had finished they polished the old dining room table and spread a white cloth over it. Soon it was laid with the most amazing festive spread: roast beef, roast chicken, potatoes, steamed vegetables, gravies, custards, jellies, ice-cream and other tit bits. Saras and I looked at all this with relish but we could not eat until mother came down. She eventually arrived. We gasped. I had forgotten how beautiful she looked.

Dressed in her favourite pink silk dress and with her stylishly coiffured hair, she revived memories of her former beauty and cheerful gait. She seated herself at the head of the table and together with the clinking of glasses and light–hearted laughter we undoubtedly felt like family again. Except for dad, he was not there, in fact he had not come home for the last three days. But I was happy and I did not wish for him to return for he had a sense of heaviness that would certainly have dispelled the festive atmosphere like the whiff of a candle. These hopeful thoughts, however, were soon banished when heavy footsteps a door flung open and the most violent profusion of verbal abuse snatched our moment of joy. The shocked and devastated looks on our faces would remain in our minds forever.

There were no words or actions that came from us, but I could sense the deep disappointment and fury that welled within us. What followed sent us into immediate shock and would be entrenched in our consciousness for the rest of our lives.

Mother approached him with a sense of renewed strength and we could not fathom this new stance. It was only when she pulled out the sword sharp carving knife from behind her back and lodged it firmly through his chest that the reality of her intentions dawned on us.

Dad did not die, instead he remains a vegetable, lying inert and useless on his bed the whole time, a constant reminder of his hopeless and wasted life. Mother spends most of her time nursing him and I spend most of my time caring for both of them. They say that I have my mother's hands and that is indisputable , but I sure do not want to have my mother's life.

Beautiful woman
By Veena Narainen

Beautiful woman ,
Lying in a slumber.
What are you dreaming about?
I think,
A far off land
With rolling green hills,
Where the nightingale sings
With the gurgling stream.
You stop to pick
A golden buttercup.
How sweet! How fresh!
How different!
You think...
Of early mornings,
Fussy routines ,
Screaming babies sitting on hips.
Tired feet , swollen hands,
servitude!
You stop...
Buttercup petal,
Against your cheek.
How gentle,
How fragrant.
Trickling springs ,
Twittering birds,

Making music.
You listen…
What's that noise?
Oh, it's you again.
Critical tones , scathing remarks.
Impatient!
Vociferous , demanding ,
Is there no room for me to grow?
Blameless!
Is my strength a weakness?
My beauty a flaw?
Why?...
It's always you ,
Threatening darkness ,
Slithering snake ,
Painfully stabbing my beautiful world.
I think…
It's cruel fate
When you awake
Life's still the same ,
Save in your dreams

You can only hope.

A NEW SEASON
By Veena Narainen

The rising sun splattered a fusion of warm colours across the sky. First a crimson hue , then a deep orange that slowly transformed into feathery patterns of soft yellow light. Below the rolling hills the sun's warmth slowly awakened the sleeping village. A rooster crowed. It was Tuesday morning.

'Thula! thula! Njalo ukhala sengi vukile , uyangicasula leqhude eligygile!' (Shut up! shut up! You are always crowing at the wrong time , you old rooster.) 'That irritating rooster, wait until I wring its scraggy neck," shouted gogo MaDuma.

As she drew in a huge breath, her eyes caught sight of a puny figure, of about seven or eight walking slowly towards her. His faded brown shirt slumped off his right shoulder and barely covered his spindly frame. As he neared his features became more apparent. His face was smeared with patches of powdery dust and his sunken cheeks gave his face a rather distorted appearance. MaDuma looked at his feet. Short, stubby toes were separated by thick cakes of mud while the length of his toenails were exaggerated by the amount of dirt that protruded from underneath it. The hapless boy stopped next to MaDuma and greeted her.

'Sawabona gogo,'

'Sawubona,' replied MaDuma.

'I've come to buy bread and milk.'

MaDuma's eyebrows creased with concern. The boy certainly needed more than bread and milk. It seemed as if he was bereft of a lifetime of nourishment, love and care.

'I haven't seen you before. Whose boy are you?'

'Nellie is my mama, gogo. My name is Mthobisi,' replied the boy.

'Yes I do remember your mother, but I have not seen her for a while. How is she?'

'My mama is very sick and can't come to your tuckshop herself.'

'What is wrong with her?'

'I don't know. She is very weak and sleeps the most of the day. Mama is not very strong. On Saturday she fell in the toilet and Lindiwe, my sister had to help her. She has to do all the work. Lindiwe said that I must get bread and milk from you, gogo.'

'Sorry, sorry, come inside,' said MaDuma apologetically as she hurried into the tuckshop. Mthobisi followed her in. MaDuma noticed how his deep set eyes widened in amazement when he looked at the freshly baked cakes and breads on the shelf and when his eyes rested on the jars of bubblegum, mint drops and assortment of goodies, a thin drizzle of saliva snaked its way from the corner of his dry lips.

'There's your bread and milk, Do you have any money?' asked MaDuma suspecting that he had none. Mthobisi shook his head as MaDuma placed a mint drop in his outstretched hand.

'Thank you gogo. Put it on account. Please give me some sweets for Lindiwe too and one for Norma , Sandile and the baby.'

'Your mama has a little baby? How old is the baby?' asked MaDuma.

'Mama does not have the baby yet, but her stomach is very big and she said that it won't be long before it comes.'

'Who is taking care of your mama?' asked MaDuma.

'Lindiwe, gogo,' replied Mthobisi in between squishy chewing of his mint drop.

'Lindiwe , but she is just a little girl?' replied MaDuma shocked.

'Lindiwe is small, but she is just like mama, gogo. She cooks for us but only when she finds something to cook. But she is getting tired and sick like mama too. In the night she falls on the bed and sleeps like she is dead.' MaDuma shook her head and fell into deep thought. She did not like what she had just heard.

'Sawubona MaDuma.' MaDuma's head jerked up from her deep reverie. It was Themba the cosmetic and shoe salesman. She had not seen him for a while.

'Sawubona Themba,' replied MaDuma sullenly and thinking that he looked very scrawnier than usual.

'What's worrying you, gogo ? I can see you are not yourself today.'

'Life is full of worries, Themba and yes I am very concerned. This boy's mother,' said MaDuma pointing to Mthobisi ,'is very sick and she has no mother to look after her. I wish I could do something. I hate to see suffering. You don't look too good yourself.'

'You are right. I haven't been well too, flu and bronchitis you know. I can take you to the boy's mother if you like,' volunteered Themba not wanting to see MaDuma so upset. He was fond of the old lady who treated him like her son.

'Ngiyabonga, thank you Themba. If it's not too much trouble.'

'No trouble at all, gogo. Let John my helper watch your shop and I'll take you right away.

'Okay, let me fetch some things and my bag' she said as she disappeared in to the tuckshop. Themba looked at the puny figure. There was something familiar about him. Where had he seen him? While he was pondering on this enigma, MaDuma appeared with her arms full of parcels.

'Come Mthobisi, take us to your mama,' she said. The old bakkie rattled along the dirt road. As the tyres grated along the stony surface, swirls of dust rose around the bakkie and covered the once white surface that blended in perfectly with the winter landscape. The road narrowed into a bumpy grind and Mthobisi pointed in its direction. MaDuma remained pensive as she stared at the bleak scenery. Clusters of mud huts dotted the foot of the hills. Some were painted in earthy tones of oranges, yellows and reds and were decorated in bold geometric shapes. MaDuma sighed loudly when she thought of the talent and potential that lay within those attractive walls.

Just then a group of barefooted children ran

along a broken down fence and waved cheerfully at them, their wide grins revealing their yellowing teeth. MaDuma waved back at them while Themba smiled at the familiar sight. He was still smiling when he brought the bakkie to an abrupt halt. Five goats bleated angrily, raised their bearded heads proudly and strutted across the road in a manner which resembled a beauty pageant and which would have taken a good deal of time, had not a furious bull come raging from across the field and cause them to hurry across rather inelegantly.

MaDuma looked at Mthobisi and they both laughed out aloud. Children should grow up with laughter, she thought, noticing how the corners of his lips curled up. Themba revved the engine and continued to drive.

'Is your mama's home far from here?' he asked Mthobisi.

' No but we have to cross the bridge by the river down there,' replied Mthobisi, pointing to the right. Themba hesitated. Not many people lived across that bridge. He knew that. He had been there many times, well until recently.

Tall bushes swished past as them arrived at their destination. In a clearing, covered by nettles and sticks was a stony pathway that led to the house. The cracks in the mud walls , like vindictive streaks of lightning extended from the sloping pieces of tin roof, past the broken window panes to the wild bushes that edged the shaky foundations. A little girl , clad only in a grey shorts and colourful plastic beads around her neck, scribbled patterns with a stick in the sand in which she sat, while a brown dog, pestered by a hungry fly, nestled its head in her lap. They looked up sharply as the bakkie stopped.

MaDuma looked at Themba. He was sweating and wiping his brows as if he had a fever.

'You not well, Themba? What's wrong?' she asked with genuine concern.

'Nothing, nothing, you go in. I'll join you just now,' said Themba in a trembling voice.

'Okay, you sure you are alright?' Themba nodded.

MaDuma pushed the door open. She followed Mthobisi in. The darkness that mingled with the sickly smell of dampness hovered heavily in the air. She nearly fell, but luckily Mthobisi held her. She bent to pick up the obstacle. It was a baby's bottle, caked with dry milk that had strands of curly hair and tiny pieces of dust stuck to it. As the darkness faded into dull light, the room became more apparent. Peeling blue paint hung alongside faded picture frames. It was sparsely furnished. Two food-stained brown couches rested against the dirty walls while a small coffee table stood on a discoloured flowery carpet in the centre. A toddler, whose head rested on the table, chewed at her orange vest.

'This is Norma,' said Mthobisi as he rubbed her head affectionately.

'Sawubona Norma,' said MaDuma as she smiled at the beautiful, but unkempt girl who stared at her blankly.

'Mama is in that room,' said Mthobisi pointing to the door on the left.

MaDuma walked stealthily to the room and peeped into the dark room. Where was Themba she thought hoping that he was fine?

On a single bed lay a gaunt figure. MaDuma noticed that her eyes, which sunk deep into her sockets, were circled by dark frames while her hollowed cheeks surrounded lips that almost disappeared into her mouth. She was certainly a vision of death.

'Sawubona , I'm gogo MaDuma,' she said to the thin figure kneeling by the bedside.

'Sawubona , I'm Lindiwe and this is my

mama,' she said while she gently swabbed the feverish sweat with a damp face towel.

'You're a very brave girl, Lindiwe, and a very good one too,' said MaDuma as she raised the pillows and helped the wraithlike body sit up using her strong hands. 'Has your mama eaten?' she asked Lindiwe.

'Not for two days, gogo. I did not have anything to give her. On Sunday I gave her a little soup but her stomach was cramping and she did not finish it. I sent Mthobisi to get milk and bread from you.'

'I know, I know', said MaDuma comfortingly as she noticed Themba stick his head in through the doorway. 'Are you better, Themba?' asked MaDuma.

Just then a frail voice called out. 'Themba, is that you? Come near so that I can see you.' Themba came closer to the bed and looked into the familiar eyes. MaDuma was shocked.

'Themba! Where have you gone to. You left me all alone. Remember you promised me..'

'Ssh…you are very sick, you must not talk,' he replied.

'No, you have done this to me. You have left me to die. You have taken away my life,' she cried bursting out in weak sobs.

' I , I...,' was all he utter as he remembered her once beautiful body that gave him many days of pleasure. But he did not expect this to happen. Not like this! Hot tears of regret stung his eyes as turned around and walked out of the room.

Sometime later MaDuma appeared. She looked around for Themba and saw him standing under the large oak tree. She looked at him. Like the heavens heavy with rain clouds, so were his eyes laden with guilt, shame and a deep sense of helplessness.

'She has not long to live,' she told him. 'When her pain would be over there would still be the children, there's still you. Poor children, with no mama to take care of them, they would be like injured animals in the wild. That is the cruel punishment of AIDS. Get yourself together, we must do something , Themba.'

Themba remained silent. He turned away from her gaze and stared at the darkening clouds that rumbled above.

Soon the fresh smell of earth permeated the air as soft rain began to fall. It was welcome, thought MaDuma to herself .The brittle bows and the monotones of the rural landscape would soon relinquish itself to the coming season. Soon the valley would flourish with colourful blossoms and lush grass while twittering birds would languish on the sweetly scented boughs.

MaDuma looked back at the children, huddled in the doorway, staring helplessly at them. Not enough rain would wash away their dark, miserable world. Even their mother's death would not release them from their pain and they would be forced to reckon with their problems and clear their own pathways.

'I'm sorry , MaDuma , I'm sorry,' sobbed Themba as he clung to her. 'I never thought that this would have happened.' MaDuma held him numbly. There were no words of comfort. Life was cruel. In its journey, no individual remained untouched by the pain and suffering, but the ability to choose wisely and make informed decisions certainly sets us above from the animal world, multiple intelligences, talented beings, progressive men and women and guardians of the earth we like to think of ourselves, but are we? Soon the season would change and bring with it new beginnings, a chance to hope , the gift of life.

WHO AM I?
By Indira Gilbert

I am a human being.
A perfect creation of God,
Made in His image.

I do have weaknesses:
Physical,
Emotional and
Psychological,
Which keep me dependent
On my Creator.

But then again,
I do have many strengths
To overcome my weaknesses.

Freedom
I gain from within,
Not from without.
How can I maintain this Freedom
Despite the world's limitations?
Through total submission
To my Creator.

THE HUMAN SPIRIT
By Indira Gilbert

There was absolute silence, observed the teacher. One could even hear a pin drop. It was as though the script in front of this group of mentally challenged children was a source of life and nourishment, all attention and energy was focused on it. Total absorption. This was the class of twenty four children with learning disabilities.

Each of them, keen to learn, attempted to give of his or her all. Unfortunately, their 'all' in the classroom did not amount to very much in every-day life, but they were passionate about the task at hand. Such commitment!

The teacher couldn't help thinking how special they were to God – blessed with compassion and love beyond one's comprehension. They were ready to smile, hug, and kiss immediately after an argument. Such child-like spirits.

Unfortunately, many of them had more than one limitation. The limited intellectual functioning was but one of their difficulties –

poor home circumstances, unemployed parents, physical and sexual abuse, alcoholism and drug addiction of parents, were among the difficulties they have had to cope with.

"Being able to cope with such insurmountable difficulties was something to be admired in itself," reflected the teacher. "Then, having to come into a school set-up and having to strain their limited intellectual ability was beyond comprehension." His admiration for them knew no bounds.

So much for the human spirit – soaring to such unbelievable heights!

FIRE
By Indira Gilbert

The garden was clean and green making quite a sight. Joe couldn't get himself to walk past a weed without destroying it. He constantly ensured that no foreign plant invaded his garden. This had become very therapeutic for him, observed his brother Nash.

Joe worked long hours at a very emotionally taxing job. Joe was a policeman, and a very passionate one at that thought Nash. Joe tried his utmost to ensure that the innocent were really protected and that the offenders were punished.

Nash knew that on returning home, Joe faced the normal family pressures. So Joe found his own, natural way of de-stressing. He would spend some time walking around his fairly large garden, nursing the plants, getting rid of the invaders, and picking up dried twigs and leaves that fell off his fruit trees. Joe would then gather the dried-up weeds and twigs into a heap. When the heap had grown to a sufficient size, Joe would get a fire going.

This fire was symbolic to Joe in many ways. It permanently got rid of invaders that destroyed his labours in the garden. It symbolized his efforts to put an end to 'invaders' to peaceful living. Furthermore, it provided warmth for his family during the cold, winter evenings. Nash watched Joe use the leaves, twigs, and dried weeds to kindle a family fire in a metal drum, where he used coal to ensure a durable fire for warmth for his family.

Joe loved his fire. He would sit around the fire with his family outside the farmhouse and toast bread for his children. In a way, it was the fire that kept Joe's family together. It was here that all family pains, joys, sorrow, and opinions were shared.

When Joe could no longer make his 'fire', Nash watched him as he sat on a stool and instructed his family members what to do. The adult children willingly submitted and kept the family 'fire' burning.

Even when Joe was no longer around, the 'fire' he had made sustained his children for a lifetime – the intimate memories of their

father, the fire, and of Joe's sharing around the
fire, kept the family 'warm'.

THE BELL OF THE ICE-CREAM MAN
By Indira Gilbert

'Ding-dong,' 'Ding-dong,' played the bell of the ice-cream van as it drove through the neighbourhood. Quickly, the children in the vicinity gathered to buy their treats.

"Mummy, it's the Ice-cream Man, Mummy, it's the Ice-cream Man," chorused Radha and Maliga. They ran towards their mother, discarding the cup and saucer set, which, up to this time, had occupied them.

Vino hurriedly wiped her floury hands on her apron as she abandoned her mixing bowl, and rushed over to the windowsill where she kept an empty lotion container as a moneybox. She grabbed the container, emptied the contents onto an old wooden bench and quickly counted the cents while the children continued in unison, "It's the Ice-cream Man, it's the Ice-cream Man."

As she re-counted the money, a look of disappointment crossed her face. There weren't sufficient cents to make up the amount required for an ice-cream cone. How

was she going to convey this disappointing news to her wide-eyed, bouncy little children? Had she not promised them on the last occasion the ice-cream man made his rounds, that she would save her monies to buy them at least one ice-cream cone?
Radha and Maliga have been given such news before. "Mummy does not have enough money, my darlings," she had told them time and time again. The ice-cream man did not come to the area often. His last visit to the area was approximately three months ago.

Vino had a lump in her throat as her mind raced rapidly through the various occasions when she had just a cent or two left from the week's wage, after attending to the family's basic needs. She had carefully placed the monies left over in this container in the windowsill to save for a treat for her two adorable children. Times were hard. Her husband's meagre salary could not make ends meet. She therefore made goodies and sold them in the neighbourhood. She always bought the cheapest groceries for use in the home just to make ends meet with a few cents to save. As she cleared the lump in her throat the children seemed to sense that something

was not right and the tone of their song "Mummy, it's the Ice-cream Man!" changed with the volume and number of repetitions having slowed down, until it ceased.
The children stood frozen, their eyes wide open, in front of Vino.

Once again she apologised that she was not able to treat them as much as she would dearly love to. Radha and Maliga ran off to the front of the tiny house without uttering a word, to watch the neighbourhood children obtaining their ice-cream treats, through the window. Vino saw Radha hug her baby sister Maliga, and heard her say, "Mummy will buy us an ice-cream cone someday, Maliga."

Hearing these words nearly broke Vino's heart. Tears ran down Vino's cheek. Yes, one day she would treat her adorable babies with an ice-cream cone. In the meantime, she would just continue loving them.

So she slipped out her apron and went to her children. She hugged them and said, "Mummy loves you!" The children seemed to have forgotten why they were in the front of the house. They hugged their mother, "We love you too, Mummy," said Radha, "and when we grow up and work, we will buy you and Daddy ice-cream cones."

Vino vowed to herself, that she would do anything to ensure that her two lovely girls would receive all the formal education possible to ensure that they might, one day, live a comfortable lifestyle. Radha and Maliga would then be able to buy their own little girls ice cream cones.

***

The years passed, and to Vino's delight, Radha and Maliga did graduate from university. Both were professionals and were fulfilling Vino's dream for a better life for them.

THE NEWSPAPER BOY
By Indira Gilbert

Marlin & Kurt were two fourteen-year old boys who grew up in the same district. Kurt came from an average socio-economic family, while Marlin came from a below-average socio-economic background. Both boys took to delivering newspapers in the neighbourhood in order to earn an income.

Marlin's family was in desperate financial circumstances. Both his parents were on social relief. The family was experiencing difficulty in sustaining a living. Marlin's income from delivering the newspapers would help pay his school fees, pay his transport to and from school, buy his school uniform, and purchase the odd stationery requirements. Not only did this job keep Marlin at school, it also helped build his self-esteem - he was partially responsible for his own upkeep. Hence his job was a source of joy to him.

For Kurt this extra income meant that he could have the extras in life which he so much aspired to a bicycle, designer clothes and shoes, extra pocket mone, and money to buy gifts for family and friends. Now he could fit-in with his peers, something he so much desired but did not want to demand off his parents who could not afford it. This job enhanced Kurt's life-style. Hence it became a source of joy for him.

Kurt became a friend to Marlin – they met while delivering papers.

One day while chatting to Marlin, Kurt learned of Marlin's reason for taking on the job of delivering newspapers. Kurt was dumbfounded. Feeling in many ways deprived of the good things in life, he did not realize that others are worse off than he is. The conversation with Marlin got him re-evaluating his own circumstances (how comfortable he really was at home) and that of others.

Kurt subsequently became very particular as to how he handled the monies he earned. No need for designer clothes and shoes, no need for extra pocket money (he would care for and wisely use what he received from his parents) and no need for expensive gifts! Kurt now saved all his earnings for when circumstances at home were not as good and he may need to purchase necessities for himself. He was now thinking of the years ahead. He planned to go to university. This would mean financial stress for his parents; considering the high cost of tertiary education. Kurt would surely need back-up money and he would have his savings.

The 'friendship' between Kurt and Marlin continued. Both had taken on a task to enrich their lives. Both had constructive plans for the use of their monies. Friendship with Marlin had indeed enriched Kurt's life. Kurt was very grateful for what he had, even if limited, in life.

***

Love,
A source of Joy
And Madness…

Where the Heart is
By Shenaaz Khan

The guide stopped dead in his tracks without
warning, because he thought he heard a faint
sound. Aman bumped into the guide
and it was only the skill and experience of the
guide that stopped him from yelling from
fright. Aman lost his bag, and he scrambled
around in the bushes and finally located his
bag amidst the brush and leaves. Behind him,
trailed three other boys, who were also being
led into the country illegally.

They trudged through the jungle for the entire
night, snacking on biscuits, sharing a water
bottle and hardly speaking, because they
knew that if the Border Rangers were to spot
or hear them, their orders were to shoot first
and ask questions later.
 Their bags were heavy, their feet were sore,
their shoulders were drooping. One young
boy, only 16, collapsed and got a very nasty
bruise from falling against the trunk of a tree.
They crossed the border between Mozambique
and South Africa in the night and after another
long walk, arrived in the city of

Gauteng. Gauteng is a hive of industries and life moves at a very fast pace there.

Aman soon spent practically all his money on necessities such as food, payment for a small room that he shared with the other boys, and calling home to assure his family that he was safe.

With his last bit of money and the clothes in his bag, he set out to seek his fortune.

He needed to earn some money and he managed to get a job at a clothing factory as a machinist. Whilst working at this factory, he met Pravesh, who was visiting Gauteng at that time. Pravesh worked in Durban, where there were many small clothing companies and he offered to take Aman with him to Durban, where he promised to get him a job. Aman did not like Gauteng very much so he agreed to go to Durban with Pravesh.

As he travelled from Gauteng to Durban in a mini bus taxi with his new friend, he closed his eyes and rested. His life had seemed like a dream, especially the last forty eight hours, and he felt if he woke up, he would be back home, in his own country, amongst his friends and family.

He would be back in his village, running
through the green fields with his friends.
They would be calling out to each other,
laughing, in the forty five degree hot sunshine.
He remembered how once they had removed
their shirts as they ran, and raced each other to
the long, winding, river.
Aman was the first to step into the water and
they began horsing around, having fun. A few
minute's later, the weather changed a little,
clouds blocked the sun. Someone playfully
tugged Aman's cap off his head.

Aman was a very handsome young man. He
was clean shaven, with high cheekbones,
almond coloured eyes and a firm jaw line.
He looked up, and in the distance, caught a
fleeting glimpse of a female figure, dressed in
white, standing in her garden, and his heart
stopped, for she was the young woman of his
dreams. The young woman he thought about
all the time, he loved her so, and she loved
him too, but he knew she was a conservative
girl living in a conservative world. There
wasn't much space for love in this world. He
had known her since she was a girl, she was
all grown up now. He had waited for this day.

Suhana lived in a huge house across the river. The river served as a divide between two communities in the village of Kusheva, a little town close to the border of Kashmir. Aman came from the poor side. He had experienced hardship very early in his life, and his was a constant battle for survival. His parents had difficulty raising him along with his two brothers and one sister. Though young and exuberant, he sometimes felt a helpless sense of despondency. He desperately wanted to escape the poverty and at the same improve the lives of his family members for the better. His family had a small rice farm and they survived on the meagre income they got from the sale of that rice in a city nearby.

Suhana, on the other hand was young, beautiful rich and spoilt. She had long lustrous black hair and large grey eyes. Her father was a land-owner, and collected rent and taxes from all the tenants, who mostly came from Aman's side of the village.
The Malhotra's home was huge and luxurious. Suhana had maids to see to her every need. She spent her days dressing up, looking pretty, entertaining her friends who were rich like she was. She was undoubtedly the most

beautiful girl in the village, and every young man's dream of the unattainable princess.

In Kusheva it was difficult to talk to a young unmarried girl without a chaperone. Aman with the help of his aunt managed to meet with her, and promised her, he would one day, equal her father in wealth and that would be the day, his parents would go over to her home and ask for her hand in marriage for their son.

Suhana promised to wait for that day.

A friend of Aman's told him about a country faraway where a lot of young people were going, in order to become rich quickly.

There were lots of jobs available and money was easy to come by, he didn't think twice. Here was his chance to become wealthy and come back to claim the woman he was determined would be his bride. With his family's blessing, he began his journey to South Africa.

The taxi arrived in the city of Durban. Aman's new friend, Pravesh was tall and thin with curly hair and brown eyes. Within a week, he was working with Pravesh in a clothing factory.

The factory he worked in, was a large and busy place. Pravesh was his supervisor and there were five other boys like Aman, who were all foreigners. They worked long hours in order to meet the demands of their employer, who in turn had to meet with the delivery date of the customer. At the end of the month, they were paid well because of the amount of work they produced. They had no family and friends to occupy them, so work was what kept them busy.

Their boss, Mr Narain, had other workers as well, who worked alongside the young men. They were South African women.

Aman was a hard worker. This quality together with his charming personality, made him a popular person. There were also people who were unfriendly and when he had difficult times, he missed home and dreamed about the day he would see his loved ones again.

He bore all his problems with patience, then somehow after two years of living in South Africa, the unthinkable happened to him. Alone, homesick and miserable, he found a friend. At first, he was curious about her, she was single and independent and seemed to have no inclination to marry. As they worked together, he found himself being drawn to her. She was reserved at first, but he set out to break her reserve. She was unresponsive for a while but finally began to melt. He found himself looking for her, whenever he walked into the factory. She was a machinist who sat across from him and it was difficult to avoid each other. Every time he looked up, he would see her lovely face and he had difficulty tearing his eyes away from her face.

She was the total opposite of Suhana. Were Suhana was tall, willowy and rich and spoilt, Alvira was petite, dainty and elegant.

She had a small face, very light brown eyes, a small straight nose and silky brown hair that fell to her shoulders. Aman noticed that she was a hard worker and he admired that quality in her.

His life had changed, and he was at a loss. He got up every morning with a feeling of anticipation, he looked forward to going to work, he would find excuses to discuss work with her. If she had to work extra hours, he would be overjoyed. He followed her every move, he knew where she was, who she talked to and found himself jealous of the other men, that she smiled at. He found himself trying to limit her interaction with other men, but she was independent and strong-willed, and he realized, he would never win her over with force.

As time went by, she continued to dominate his mind. He thought about her all the time, he couldn't believe he was falling in love, and he came to the shocking realization, that he had never felt this way before. He was so aware of her presence and he knew she was becoming aware of him and the peculiar chemistry that seemed to draw them closer to each other. He was being swept along helplessly on a tide of emotion.

He told her how he felt and she was upset because he was a foreigner and she was afraid to trust him. Eventually, he wore her resistance down. Alvira told him she had never met anyone like him before. He was magnetic, persistent and so very determined. She finally admitted to loving him. His boyish charm, his loneliness, his strength of will, all of it attracted her to him. Alvira made Aman feel strangely at peace and yet was responsible for the turmoil he was in. She was the first thing on his mind every morning and the last thing on his mind, at night, before he fell asleep. He spent the major part of his day, looking at her and still never got tired of seeing her. They sometimes had problems communicating with each other. He was Kushevan and she was South African. Their ways of thinking were vastly different.

From time to time, Aman would feel like he had withdrawn from her, fighting his own private battle. He was torn between the woman he had left behind and the woman who was now haunting him day and night.

Then one night, Aman received a message from his family in Kusheva, his father was very sick and he had to go back home.
 He had to make a quick decision, but there really was no choice. If he went back home to Kusheva, it would be a single ticket. He could not come back to South Africa because he was not a legal citizen. He phoned Alvira and told her his news, she asked to meet him. She said little after hearing his story, obviously realizing she could not change his mind. She said her heart was heavy, but she wished him well.
 As Aman looked down at the country he was leaving, tears were running freely own his face. He was leaving one love for another.

The pull of his hoe, his family, his country was too strong. He jumped off the plane and ran along the familiar village roads, joy and sorrow in his heart. He had come home.

Why do I love you?
By Shenaaz Khan

Why do I love you?
Let me think about it
I love you because
You lift me high
Higher than I've ever
Been lifted before
You make laugh
In my darkest moments
I love you because
You infuriate me

And I know, when this happens
That with you, all my senses
Are more alert than ever
You can bring me to the pits
Or the heights
But most of all
I find myself Loving you
For being there constantly
For making me feel special
And cherished

Maybe, this love will never
Be realized
But my life is richer for

Knowing you
For Loving you
For longing to be with you
To hear your voice
I am so glad
I had a chance
To experience
More than just an existence .

Heart–break
By Shenaaz Khan

I look around
And all I can see
Are reminders of you
My love, My life

How I wish that
I could see you
Just once more
Why, I don't know ?
Silent tears roll down
My cheeks, sobs wrack
My body, I dream
Of our good times
While I stare into
A bleak future
Of No you and Me
A future of emptiness .

Stars do not weep
By Shenaaz Khan

Stars do not weep
Do not shed
Your silvery tears
Do not lose your lovely lustre
Though one of you has fallen
He will return someday
For now he's visiting
Another world, another place
He had to go, you know
The command came from above
He's going to learn, to help,
To love, to live, to hurt
But when he comes back
He will be brighter,
Wiser, Special and at peace

Except, he'll have left behind
People, of Flesh and Blood and Emotions
Who weep tears of blood
Sobs that wrench at the heart
If only they would look up
They would be able to see you
Shining down on them
Smiling down at them
If only , they would look
With their hearts

A Special Kind Of Love
By Shenaaz Khan

I wish I could tell you
What your friendship means to me
You don't have a clue
But I wish you could see
If the words do not leave my lips
It's only my silly fears
That make me keep a grip
On my emotions, my laughter, my tears
I only hope that someday
You will discover and know
That even, if we're far away
My memories of you will have a
Special glow
Of something precious and pure
Like the milky way above,
That I know will endure
A special kind of love

Why do we have to care?
By Shenaaz

Why do we have to care?
Sometimes life isn't fair

Why is there so much heart-ache
Widening like ripples in a lake
We never realised , never thought
That even at times when we fought

The feelings we had were strong
It couldn't possibly be wrong
When the time came for a split
None of the pieces ever fit

Now we know for sure
What we needed was more
Time with each other, to spend
Why did it all abruptly end.

A SPECIAL FIND
By Indira Gilbert

It was a freezing winter's evening in the
countryside where the winters were bitterly
cold. One couldn't remain outdoors without
the necessary protection offered by a jacket, a
hat, and a pair of gloves. The family members,
father, mother, big brother Sagren, Sugendren,
and two younger sisters Shalena and Shareen,
had all settled in front of the large coal stove,
each with a cup of hot homemade soup as was
usual on such evenings. Sugendren always
enjoyed these times together. This was special
family time when the family could give
themselves to one another and share the
happenings of the day. Sugendren's father did
not have the privilege to share all such
evenings with the family as he worked shifts.
This was one of the special evenings when his
father was with his family.
Big brother, as usual, dominated the
conversation by relating all the exciting teen
activities and experiences. He had his own
special way of relating his experiences,
keeping his younger siblings spell-bound: they

were taken by his stories – were they really his?

Sugendren was still in primary school. He looked up to his older brother as a hero, and enjoyed his tales. Sugendren was a warm, loving personality who unquestioningly accepted whatever his big brother had to say. Sugendren needed to relieve himself. He reluctantly left the warm, cosy kitchen, and the treasured family time, and ventured outdoors with his arms folded tightly against his thick, fur jacket to prevent the cold from getting in. He hurried along to his destination (the outdoor toilet which was a couple of metres away from the house) but was startled by the sound of the chirping of a baby chick to its mother. He stopped. The cry subsided. He took a step forward. The cry was once again heard.

Sugendren loved God's creation – the birds and the animals. He cared for the family's chickens and dogs. He forgot his mission and the bitter cold he was exposing himself to. He stood still, and listened, until he was able to locate the direction from which the sound was coming.

He stepped forward. The sound became louder. He realized that the sound came from behind the house. Sugendran stepped into a less dense patch of the bush: two tiny beaded eyes reflected the light of the torch he had taken out from the pocket of his jacket. The baby chick cried out timidly. After removing his glove Sugendren stretched out his opened hand. The chick walked right into it as though it had been calling out and waiting for Sugendren. There were no signs of fear or doubt in the tiny, black chick.

Sugendren was excited. He had rescued something that had become his pet. His trip to the convenience had been forgotten. He held the chick underneath his jacket and ran to the family with his find: a black baby chick that had strayed from its mother. The family gathered around to view his find. Sugendren was excited beyond comprehension – he was a rescuer – he had rescued a pet.

As resourceful as usual, his father found a box with some warm lining. Sugendren set the box close to the heated, coal stove to enable the chick's quick recovery from the effects of the bitter cold. Sugendren now has his own, exciting experience to relate (after first visiting the convenience, off course).

He decided that the pet must be named, in keeping with the tradition of naming pets. The family together pondered over various names – it was an opportunity for them to once again work together, to make a family decision. Each family member had a contribution: each name suggested had a special meaning. Various names and their meanings were considered. Sugendren chose his father's contribution. Sugendren proudly named his new pet 'Moses'.

Sugendren asked his father to once again tell the family the story of 'Moses' as related in the Bible. "To protect baby Moses from the Egyptians who sought to murder all babies," his father began, "his mother and sister placed him in a comfortable basket. They left the basket in the river, which the Egyptian royalty frequented in the hope that one of them would rescue him and care for him. Moses' sister Miriam was given the task to watch over Moses from a 'safe' spot. As somewhat expected, the Egyptian royal took the baby Moses and nurtured him as her very own: as a royal. Moses was saved, protected and trained for a great task in life."

Was this new pet named 'Moses' also saved for some special task? wondered Sugendren.

This really did not matter. Sugendren had saved a tiny bird from certain death. It was now his special pet. He would protect it, and care for it.

"On reaching adulthood," his father continued, "Moses helped deliver the Israelites from Egyptian bondage. He saved his own people from slavery and certain death."

The pet, Moses, turned out to be a rooster. With the special 'mothering' he received from Sugendren, he soon became part of the family. While his father slept during the day after working the night shift, Moses would sleep on top of his blanket. When father awoke, Moses would then go out to be with the other chickens. Moses befriended the family's dog. Together they would relax at Dad's side during the day while Sugendren was at school.

Sugendren's father had many chickens, but Moses was special. He was the only chicken 'mothered' and the only chicken given a name. Sugendren's father actually bred chickens on his little 'farm'. One day, one of the hens which was 'sitting' on its eggs to have them hatch, was caught by a wild cat and eaten. Sugendren supposed that the poor thing could not escape as it refused to leave its eggs and 'run for cover'. His father was disappointed at the loss. It was only a week before the eggs were due to hatch.

Moses seemed to sense the father's disappointment and he voluntarily took over the 'sitting' on the eggs until they hatched. Was Sugendren excited! Moses sat on the eggs just like a hen-on-brood would do, until the eggs hatched. The job did not end when here. The chicks had to be mothered. What better way to repay a family who saved him and nurtured him? So, to Sugendren's amazement, his pet rooster became their 'mother'. This task he diligently undertook until the chicks were fully-grown and independent.

On completing this special task, Moses returned to sitting on Sugendren's father's blanket while his father slept during the day after working through the night.

So, thought Sugendren, the chick, Moses, was saved for a special task, after all.

***

Silent Love
By Valarie Chetty

A lack of love is a delusion of the mind,
Don't let it affect you.
The mind wavers.
It is a raging sea,
And a still lake.
Tame the water,
Tame the mind.
Seek the stillness of the pool,
In silence and imagination.
Float in space,
And fly in the air.
The universe is cool and dark,
But lit up with beautiful stars.
Let this be your solace,
It is there that you belong,
Alone with the stars,
At one with the universe.
Not here fumbling,
Trying to find
What's not there
In your deceptive mind
Of troubled storms.
Seek peace,
Seek me.
I am here.
Seek nothing,
For I am everything.
***

The Power
of
Emotions …

Existence
By Valarie Chetty

I'm lying on the floor,
I'm bleeding.
Looking up at the sky,
The ceiling.
I can feel the blood running out of me,
Like riotous refugees to a place of safety,
Out of this body that torments me.
Out, out, leave me.
Take the dark flames of fear, fright and pain
with you
When you run like scared children in the dark
of night.
Let the death cover me,
Take me into the darkness.

Only peace, only quiet, only numb.
Fervent sirens screaming like maddened
banshees
Shrieking though an eerie sky,
The shrill voice of deathbringing violence.
Louder and louder, and louder still.
The buzzing, the screeching and the virulous
screams of a turbulent end.

It's 5 a.m. Great, another day and I'm still
here,
Still waiting, still existing.
Only dreaming.
The prying eyes of an inquisitive sun
Creeps through my black curtains
Like a sickening witch waiting behind a veil of
darkness
To pounce on an unsuspecting newt,
To pull out its eyes and throw it into the brew.
With a surreptitious smile and malevolent
stare,
She scorches my nightloving eyes
With her jealous glare.
Staring at me the entire day,
Just watching me, mocking me and scorning
me
With her fiery arms reaching out to me.

Every day is a struggle,
For someone out in the world,
Every day is a struggle.

I'm walking down the road.
Everything is still crisp from the nightcold air,
The ground still wet with morning dew.
I take a deep breath in.
I can just feel the brittle air flow through me,

Sharply down my nostrils and into my brain,
Awakening.
Another deep breath,
And slowly the icy crystals suffocate me.
Every breath wants to kill me.
To live is to die.
Slowly, with each day we live,
With each day we die.
Little by little,
Cell by cell we are dying,
Just wasting away.

I wonder what it's like to die...
Is it like going to bed and just never waking
up?
Is it like a dream?
Does your soul leave your body and journey
somewhere?
Is there a somewhere?
Do we even have a soul?
Or maybe, it's just nothingness,
Like before you were born.
Do you go back to where you came from?
From nowhere,
Just a body that began
And now a body that ends?

I'm waiting.

There's always a long wait.
We waste so much time waiting.
Just waiting.
We wait for people,
We wait for taxis,
We wait for opportunities,
We wait in queues,
We wait for results,
We even wait for time.
Waiting is such a waste.
There's so much I could be doing instead of
waiting here for a damn taxi!
I could be doing something productive!
Why are you wasting my time?
IT'S SO FRUSTRATING!
I'm getting irritable.
Would you just get here!!!
I have things to do!

I can feel the blood in my veins start to scurry.
Even they're starting to get restless.
All trying to find a way out,
Out of this long wait.
Where to go?
Round and round,
Nowhere but where they've been before.
At least they're not wasting time doing
nothing!

They're clamouring on top of each other,
Trying to burst out,
Out of this finite state,
Out of this incessant wait.
Finally,
a break.
They burst somewhere out,
A flood of blood rushing to freedom,
Somewhere out of this frustration.
I think I've burst a vessel.

I'm lying on the floor.
I'm bleeding.
Looking up at the sky,
Inside my head.
Al I can see is red.
There's a drip,
There's a leak.
I'm feeling...
Nothingness.
I'm feeling nothing.
I cant move,
I cant do anything,
Except breathe.
The inability to move,
To do something,
To get something done,
To do something about the inability to move,

Is killing me.

I can feel the great beast inside me awaken.
Something stirs the devil that is me.
Something unleashes a terrible fever that
burns me.
It's anger,
Its frustration,
Its stress,
It's everything that the world gives me.
Everything that the world gives me wants to
kill me.
A raging fire boiling to the brim,
With violent hatred,
Red-hot and fiery.
Dying with a vengeance,
The world has killed me.
I am killed me.

What I am,
Has killed me.

***

Pain
By Shenaaz Khan

Pain, consistent , never far away
How unlike joy, that is fleeting
But yet pain is welcomed by some
Abhorred by others
You can't quite escape
You can fight, you can resist
Whether you win or lose
Is a mixture of strength, luck
And the Will of the Almighty.

Bitterness wells up
By Shenaaz Khan

Bitterness wells up
In my mouth
Like bile, foul tasting
Making me gag
Why do I let things
Affect me so much
When others strike
With sharp words

Like swords that cut
Deep into my soul
And never care
To mend the deep wound
Soon all is forgiven
The memory fades
The wounds heals
Only the scar's remain .

A yearning
By Shenaaz Khan

A yearning, a craving
For something
I know not what
Or is it that
I do know
But refuse to acknowledge
What I know

So suppressed are we
By society and it's
Unreasonable blind rules
That our head rules
Where in fact
Our heart is king
But we're afraid
Of things intangible

Of the unknown
Of life, of death
Of taking a chance
And so we wish
And dream
And long
For something we are
Afraid to go out and get.

My Wall Of Fear
By Shenaaz Khan

What is this fear I cannot express
Why do I hold back, my
Feelings repress
I wish I could set my
Feelings free
Laugh , in abandon , in glee

But I'm bound by chains
Too afraid of getting hurt,
Afraid of pain
So what will be my fate
Or will I find a way past
This wall when it is too late.

Breaking that shell
By Shenaaz Khan

My mind running round in circles
Chasing shadows, chasing dreams
I will not be constrained anymore
I am breaking that shell
I will emerge free
Vulnerable, capable of getting hurt
The shell doesn't allow me
To feel, it protects,
But it leaves me closed up.

Vulnerable, proud, happy
I am stepping forth
I place myself in God's hands
He never asked for us
To live in a bubble
There's always space
Between me and the next person
I am closing the gap
I pray, if I get hurt, I will be stronger.

Here I sit alone
By Shenaaz Khan

Here I sit alone
Yet not alone
I'm surrounded by people
Who speak, laugh , eat
I hear music
And strangely enough
I'm not alone
For loneliness comes with unhappiness
As long as you're not content with yourself
If you cannot find the quiet place
Deep within your very self
As long as you don't have faith
In your strength, in your abilities
And your courage
If you can look at yourself
Take a good, long , hard look
And still have the ability to respect yourself
If you have pride in your achievements
Whether it concludes in success or
Failure
If you believe and your belief is
Unshakeable
You are home, you are free
You are a whole person.

Destiny
By Shenaaz Khan

I try to escape
The sound of thunder
I clap my hand
Over my ears
No matter where I turn
Death follows me
Grim -faced, but giving me
Welcome relief, from misery .

Indecision
By Shenaaz Khan

Swirling mist surrounds me
And I look around in fear
How do I find my way
What if I lose direction
I wonder, I can see through
The mist
Two roads, left, and right
Which turn should I take
Indecisiveness grips me
If I take the first turn
I will be heading towards
A lot of joy, love and happiness
Heading towards someone
Who has given me a lot of
Love and caring
I'm afraid the joy
Will turn to sorrow, the
Love to hate
If I take the second turn
I will be heading towards
Safety and security, a comfort zone
I'm afraid the safety and security
Could lead to loneliness, bitterness
And regret.

"The fabric of society is a tapestry of cultures, A web of beautiful colours blending into one another."

Valarie Chetty

PRECIOUS FREEDOM
by Indira Gilbert

'Free at last, Free at last!'
Words priceless to those bound in the past.
Years and years of precious time
Wasted.
Creativity stumped.
Growth stagnated.
Movement controlled.
Life lived in submission to mortal man.

'Free at last, Free at last'
To be whatever one dreams of,
To do whatever the mind can invent,
To go wherever one desires.
The sky is the limit,
One can reach for the stars.
The only limitation is
Submission to the Immortal.

'Free at last, Free at last.'
How is this precious Freedom handled?
Do we succumb to our own vices
Of alcohol, drugs, and promiscuity?
Are we losing the Freedom
So passionately fought for?

'Free at last, Free at last'
These may soon become
Words of the past!

SOCCER:
By Indira Gilbert

"Come. Come. Come. Over here……. John, pass…pass".

The excitement, stress, absorption in the game of soccer was ever present, even after a long, tiring day at work. So real were the experiences of the players on the field that the field came alive with all the cheering, roaring and screaming of the spectators.

A player took the ball at the defence end, and dribbled all the way to the scoring end. The crowd roared, his team members ran to support him, but alas the ball was lost to the opposition. His team supporters went silent.

Supporters of the opposition team roared.

The match was nearing the end. Stress was building up for both players and supporters alike. Supporters were willing and ready to argue, fight and squeal, just to see victory for their team.
Each pass of the ball was cheered or jeered.
Bottles, cans and other items were in some

instances thrown onto the field. There was such an adrenalin rush: other supporters of the same team become friends while friends who supported the opposite team became rivals. For the players, team members were friends while members of the opposite team were foes.

With the match being over, within a couple of minutes the sports field became a peaceful haven for all those who lived in close proximity. Friends once again became friends.

If only sports fields could talk!

***

Thoughts on war
By Valarie Chetty

It's a wonder how,
The world is so bitter now…
Brothers feed the darkening clouds,
With the blood of their kin.

From dust to dust,
Through hatred and lust.
The earth is a burning flame.
An imminent explosion
Of atrocious desires,
Throw all your hopes into the pyres.

One full circle,
Of power and might.
One more day and one less night.

Look into the mirror of your souls,
The quickening deluge takes us all.
It's not up to you…
You are
Only human,
But then again,
You really couldn't be.

Letter to the Queen (of England)
By Valarie Chetty

You sit there on your high throne,
With diamonds on your crown,
Gotten from working my brothers to the bone.

You sit there and dictate,
Point your finger at the globe,
(This must surely be a place you hate)
Saying, "Ah this village I will pillage, plunder
and probe!
What political and economic institutions I
create,
Let no primitive decimate!"

Money, money, money makes the world go
round,
Falling shillings, pennies and pounds,
Ah, what a marvellous sound!
Blocking out the cries
Of starving children burdened with flies,
Damn children of the Earth,
Let them eat dirt!
Drive their souls deep into the ground
And let no evidence ever be found!

You sit there on your high throne,
Come down oh adorable queen,
With your precious jewels dripping
Like the glistening tears and sweat
That got them 'round your royal neck.

Come down, oh adorable queen,
Walk with your bare feet on solid ground,
Run with the wild animals on the planes
And let your soul soar on the back of an eagle
And see the games our children play
Come down oh adorable queen,
And let the Earth be queen for a day.

Perpetual Liminality
By Valarie Chetty

I'm in a state of perpetual liminality,
Being post-colonial is no fun.
I don't know who I am
Or where I'm from!

A victim of ecocide,
You ruined my land.
You stole my trees,
My animals,
And my Earth.

A victim of ethnocide,
You ruined my culture.
You stole my language,
My religion
And my soul.

A victim of genocide,
You ruined my life.
You stole my people,
My family,
My future
And everything else that makes me whole.

Now I'm in a state of perpetual liminality,
Neither here nor there.
Neither Indian nor African,
Somewhere in-between,
But neither can ever fully be seen.

My Africa
By Valarie Chetty

Let my spirit soar,
On the back of an eagle.
Flying high,
Across the beautiful African sky.
Past the burning, breathing, fiery mountains
Of my land.

Let the smoke cover my eyes,
And blind me to the truth I see.
My brothers and sisters,
Wash their faces in muddy waters
Of the flowing rivers
That run to the sea.

Ignorant of the world around them
Only knowing what is needed.
Not longing for price or fame,
Not wanting the highlights of a neon-lit name.

Only existing,
Dwelling on this earth,
With lives still whole.
Still this primal scream,
It captures my soul

This is *my* Africa.
***

Two men caught my attention
By Shenaaz Khan

Two men caught my attention
As I sat on the cold bench
At the Railway station
Waiting for the morning train
A beggar , who was dressed in
Rags , no shoes , trying hard to
Keep the winter chill at bay
By holding those rags
Close to his body

The other , a well-dressed Man
Obviously on his way to work
Carrying a briefcase under his arm
All warm and snug in a huge coat , a hat on his
head , shoes
To protect his feet .

Their paths cross , the beggar
Whines , grovelling in a manner
That makes me cringe
The Well – Dressed Man , looks
At him in contempt
Tells him to go and work
For his money

Both are Men hardened by
Their situations
Men who could otherwise
Have been friends

But never will be

The Black Executive
And the White Beggar .

Dirt
By Shenaaz Khan

Dirt, filth, voices raised in
Raucous laughter, all around
The sound of machines
Roaring in my ears.
I hear a call, I turn, I hear
Another , I turn again,
The calls increase, I cover
My ears in confusion.

What am I doing here in
This place so foreign to
My dreams and wishes
What price money when it
Is at the expense of
One's sweat, toil and tears.

*****

The classroom
By Veena Narainen

Mischievous eyes,
laughing aloud,
winking at each other
as if they know…
Now is the time,
why wait for tomorrow
for fun, fun , fun?

Tapping feet, restless fingers,
tickle and prod
giggling girls,
bashful boys.
Scraping on desks,
scribbling on walls,
nobody dares to
complain!
Nobody cares to
restrain.
The chaotic crescendo,
deafeningly enjoyable,
unbearable,
until…
heavy footsteps,
come closer , closer,
then,
SILENCE!

www.ingramcontent.com/pod-product-compliance
Lightning Source LLC
Chambersburg PA
CBHW050410030726
47503CB00006B/2128